READING

RECOVERY

An I Can Read Book®

HERE COMES ◆◆◆ THE ◆◆◆ STRIKEOUT

Leonard Kessler

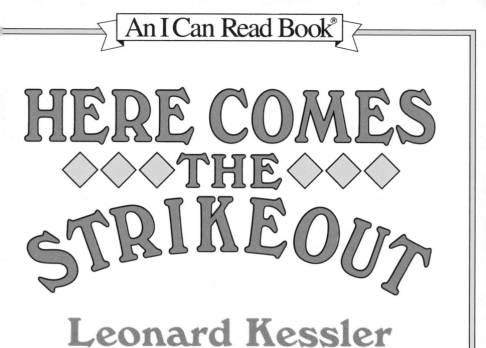

HarperTrophy
A Division of HarperCollins*Publishers*

Here Comes the Strikeout
Copyright © 1965, 1992 by Leonard Kessler
Printed in the U.S.A. All rights reserved.
Newly Illustrated Edition
Published in hardcover by HarperCollins Publishers.

Library of Congress Cataloging-in-Publication Data
Kessler, Leonard P., date
  Here comes the strikeout / by Leonard Kessler.
    p.   cm. — (An I can read book)
  Summary: Bobby changes from an "easy out" to a game-winning hitter
with the help of a friend and a lot of hard work.
  ISBN 0-06-444011-7 (pbk.)
  [1. Baseball—Fiction.] I. Title. II. Series.
PZ7.K484He   1992b   91-14720
[E]—dc20   CIP
                                                                AC

TO MY FAVORITE BASEBALL PEOPLE

OF YESTERDAY AND TODAY:

Arky Vaughan	Mickey Mantle
Pie Traynor	Matt Nicholas Kessler
Paul Waner	Benson Ansell
Casey Stengel	Jake Fishman
Willie Mays	Sue Carr Hirschman

In the spring

the birds sing.

The grass is green.

Boys and girls

run to play

BASEBALL.

Bobby plays baseball too.

He can run the bases fast.

He can slide.

He can catch the ball.

But he cannot

hit the ball.

He has *never*

hit the ball.

11

"Twenty times at bat

and twenty strikeouts,"

said Bobby.

"I am in a bad slump."

12

"Next time try my
good-luck bat,"
said Willie.
"Thank you," said Bobby.
"I hope it will help me
get a hit."

"Boo, Bobby,"

yelled the other team.

"Easy out.

Easy out.

Here comes the strikeout."

"He can't hit."

14

"Give him the fast ball."

Bobby stood at home plate

and waited.

The first pitch

was a fast ball.

"Strike one."

The next pitch

was very slow.

Bobby swung hard,

but he missed.

"Strike two."

"Boo! Strike him out!"

"I will hit it this time,"

said Bobby.

He stepped out

of the batter's box.

He tapped the lucky bat

on the ground.

He stepped back
into the batter's box.
He waited for the pitch.

It was a fast ball

right over the plate.

Bobby swung.

"STRIKE THREE!

You are OUT!"

The game was over.

Bobby's team had

lost the game.

"I did it again," said Bobby.

"Twenty-one times at bat.

Twenty-one strikeouts.

Take back your lucky bat, Willie.

It was not lucky for me."

It was not a good day

for Bobby.

He had missed

two fly balls.

One dropped out

of his glove.

And one went

over his head.

He had struck out three times.

And his team

had lost the game.

He walked home alone.

"How was the game?"

asked his mother.

"Oh, it was fine,"

said Bobby.

"Time for a nice hot bath,"

said his mother.

Bobby went to take his bath.

He sat in the tub.

He was not happy.

"Twenty-one times at bat.

Twenty-one strikeouts,"

he said.

And then he began to cry.

"Are you all right in there?"

called his mother.

"I am fine," cried Bobby.

"Then why are you crying?"

asked his mother.

"I'm not crying,"

said Bobby.

"What is the matter, then?"

asked his mother.

"Oh, every time I play baseball,

all I do is strike out.

No one wants me

on the team.

"They even choose

the little kids

before they choose me.

They always choose me last."

He sobbed again.

"I wish I were a good hitter."

"You can be a good hitter,"

said his mother.

"You are a good swimmer.

You are a good runner.

You must work until

you are a good hitter."

"Maybe Willie will help me.

He is a good hitter.

I will ask him," said Bobby.

"Good," said his mother.

"And one more thing.

Did you wash

your face and your ears?"

The next day

Bobby went to see Willie.

"Sure I will help you

with your hitting,"

said Willie.

"But you must work hard

every day.

Lucky helmets won't do it.

Lucky bats won't do it.

Only hard work will do it."

"I will work hard,"

said Bobby.

"I want to be a good hitter."

"First we must choose
a bat for you.
We will choose one that is
not too heavy, not too light,
not too long, but just right.

"First you hold the bat

this way,

keep your feet

this way,

and you swing the bat
this way, see.

Now you try it."

Bobby did it.

And he did it again

and again

and again.

"One more time,"
said Willie.

"Keep your eyes
on the ball.
Just try to meet
the ball with the bat.
Don't swing too hard.
Just meet it."
Willie pitched the ball.
Bobby swung the bat
very hard.

He swung so hard
that he fell down.

"Strike one,"

said Willie.

"Let's try it again.

But swing easy."

Willie pitched the ball again.

Bobby swung.

And this time

he hit the ball!

He did not hit it very far,

but he hit the ball.

"Good hit," said Willie.

"You hit it.

You did it."

"I HIT THE BALL.

I HIT THE BALL,"

shouted Bobby.

"I CAN DO IT.

I CAN GET A HIT!"

He jumped up and down.

"Let's try it again,"

said Willie.

And that is what they did

all that day,

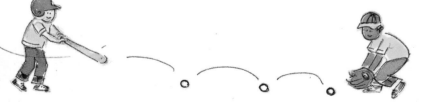

and the next day,

and the next.

Some days Bobby

worked with Willie.

Some days he

worked alone.

39

Some days he did

a little better.

Some days he did not

do so well.

There were good days.

There were bad days.

But he kept working and trying.

"I hope I get a hit

in a game," said Bobby.

"You can hit the ball,"

said Willie.

"You will get a hit

in a game."

SPECIAL

BIG
CONE

7

FLAVORS

The next day

was a big game.

Bobby's team was the Bobcats.

The other team was the Sluggers.

The first time Bobby came to bat,

he did everything

Willie had told him.

He was ready!

The first pitch was a strike.

On the next pitch Bobby swung.

And he hit the ball.

It was a little pop fly

to the shortstop.

Bobby was out.

"But I hit it,"

said Bobby.

"I will do better next time."

At the bottom

of the fourth inning

the score was

    Sluggers: Three runs

    Bobcats: Three runs

Then Willie came up to bat.

He hit a long drive

to center field.

"Home run, home run!"

yelled his team.

But a little dog

ran off with the ball.

They had to stop

the game and chase the dog

to get the baseball back.

48

Then both teams had to rest

from all that running.

It was a long inning.

In the last inning

the score was still

Sluggers: Three runs

Bobcats: Three runs

	1	2	3	4	5	6	R	H	E
SLUGGERS	0	1	0	2	0	0			
BOBCATS	0	0	3	0	0				

It was the last time

at bat for the Bobcats.

There were two outs.

There was a runner on third base.

And who was up at bat?

It was Bobby.

"Look who is up,"

yelled the Sluggers.

"HERE COMES THE STRIKEOUT!"

"Move in close. He can't hit it."

"Strike him out."

Bobby held the bat.

"I can do it,"

he said softly.

He swung

and missed.

"Strike one."

"Move in closer,"

shouted the shortstop.

"He was lucky

the last time up.

He can't hit it again."

Bobby swung.

"Strike two."

"One more strike

and he is out."

The shortstop laughed.

Willie walked up to the plate.

"Get a hit, Bobby.

Just meet the ball,"

said Willie.

"You can do it!"

The pitcher looked over

at the runner on third base.

He looked at Bobby.

And now he was ready.

The pitch came in fast.

Bobby swung his bat.

CRACK.

POW.

Up—up.

Up went the ball

over the head of the shortstop

and dropped on the grass.

It was a base hit.

"Run, Bobby. Run to first base!"

yelled Willie.

Bobby just stood there.

"Run! Run! Run!"

the Bobcats screamed.

Bobby started to run.

He ran fast.

"Safe!"

The runner on third base

had crossed home plate

with the winning run.

The game was over.

The Bobcats had won.

"Good hit, Bobby,"

said Willie.

"Good hit,"

said the other Bobcats.

"Twenty-three times at bat.

Twenty-one strikeouts,

one pop fly,

and ONE HIT."

Bobby smiled at Willie.

When he came home

his mother asked,

"How was the game?"

Bobby smiled.

"I got a hit.

We won the game."

"Wonderful!" said his mother.

Now when Bobby plays baseball,

sometimes he strikes out.

But most times he hits the ball.

"How do you do it?" asked Matt.

"A lucky bat?" asked Sally.

"No," said Bobby.

"Lucky bats won't do it.

Lucky helmets won't do it.

Only hard work will do it."

Bobby looked at Willie,

and they laughed.